The Serpent and the Swallow

A Curses of Never Prequel

Printed in the United States of America: First Printing, 2024

ISBN 978-1-960411-09-9 (paperback)

ISBN 978-1-960411-08-2 (ebook)

Published by Night Muse Press

Edited by Nastasia Bishop in collaboration with Stardust Book Services

Formatted by R. L. Davennor

NIGHT MUSE PRESS

EST. 2020

Acknowledgements

You know what? This one's for me.
To all the sleepless nights,
the countless days I spent lonely and alone.
To all the times I convinced myself
that I wouldn't make it, that no one
was reading my stories,
and that no one was coming to save me.
To how wrong I was,
because I saved myself.
Oh—and to you too, Elvira.
Your insanity kept me sane.

ALSO BY R. L. DAVENNOR:

The Curses of Never Series:

*** A Dance with the Devil*

*** The Serpent and the Swallow*

A Land of Never After

A Sea of Eternal Woe

A Forest of Blackened Trees

A River of Tormented Souls

The Phantom of Notre Dame Series:

The Hells of Notre Dame

The Masque of Crimson Shadow

The Spectre of Moonless Night

Standalones:

Dragon Lake: A Swan Lake Retelling

*** – denotes prequel novella*

To any bisexual person who's ever experienced erasure:
Your sexuality is not determined by the gender of your partner.
I see you.

Before You Begin:

If you are new to the Curses of Never series, **I do not recommend beginning with this novella.** While the events depicted take place prior to the events of book one, *A Land of Never After*, prior knowledge of the world, its characters, and lore is highly recommended (and I would argue necessary) for full enjoyment.

My suggested reading order is as follows:
A Land of Never After
A Dance with the Devil
A Sea of Eternal Woe
The Serpent and the Swallow

For the ambitious reader, reading *A Land of Never After* alone *may* be enough context for this to make sense to you - but again, I do not recommend it.

Please also note that this novella contains graphic depictions of violence, language, mentions of depression and suicide, explicit sexual content, medium to heavy knife play, including insertion (by the handle), and is intended for a mature adult audience.

"Do you know," Peter asked, "why swallows build in the eaves of houses? It is to listen to the stories."
- J. M. Barrie, *Peter Pan*

I. THE WOUND

My brother flinched, my hand slipped, and I wanted to fucking scream.

Alcohol poured freely down his back, completely missing the wound I was attempting to clean and redress. Though I'd barely touched him, obscenities poured from his lips, colorful even for his standards. "Gently, damn it, and be careful!"

"Careful?" I slammed the bottle on his desk, nearly shattering it, but if Cedric was going to be a reckless ass, so was I. "You're one to talk about *careful* when you're the one wasting all our rum."

He shot me such a venomous glare that anyone else would no doubt have winced or cowered beneath its weight. The numerous scars marring his face only added to the hateful illusion, but my brother would have to try far harder than that if he truly wanted to scare me. "I'll get right on healing my own infection, then," he hissed through gritted teeth.

"I'd settle for you letting me heal it. By *not* leaping out of your skin every time I get anywhere near you."

Cedric grunted something unintelligible, and taking it as a sign we were both exhausted from this bickering, I returned to my work, slower this time. Before I could even raise a rag to wipe him off though, a voice piped up from the far corner.

"He's getting worse." Scarlett, my brother's… lover? Partner? I didn't know precisely what to call her, especially now that they were sleeping in separate quarters, but just like the rest of us occupying this sorry excuse for a ship, Scarlett didn't have anywhere else to go. She met my gaze from where she crouched in the shadows, but didn't otherwise move. "He tries to trivialize and lie about his pain, but he's in quite a lot of it."

Fuck. Equal parts fear and worry rose in my throat, but I kept my expression impassive as I turned back to Cedric. "Is that true?"

He hesitated, which was an answer in itself, so I fixated on the wound marring his back. What should have healed months ago was now a festering, gaping hole. Infected, yes, but even that was putting it mildly. Angry black lines snaked outward from its edges, crisscrossing Cedric's already scarred skin like an intricate map, and the surrounding flesh was swollen and red. Heat radiated from him in waves, and when he glanced over his shoulder, I noted the sweat pooling at his brow. *Gods damn it, now he's feverish on top of everything else?*

"You look like shit, and you smell even worse," I said, but only to mask how terrified I was. Internally, I stifled a scream yet again, because this was serious, far more than I'd previously allowed myself to believe. Cedric's only response was a faint grunt, confirming my suspicions and far more. "And you've been killing? This isn't a result of the curse?"

"It can't be," Scarlett answered, at last rising to her feet and taking a small step forward. "Since he's been too weak to leave the ship, I've ensured he's had plenty of rat necks to snap. The rot heals, but his wound doesn't."

At the mention of decaying flesh, my own pain flickered to life. The worst of it may be concealed beneath several layers of clothing, but like everyone and everything else in this fucking forest, I was rotting, too. Such was Neverland's curse, accidentally set off the same day Cedric had been stabbed, perhaps even the same moment. *Death pays for death*, which in simpler terms meant kill or decay. We were all actively festering from the inside out. Murder was the only thing that reversed the rot, but only for a week at most. It had been four days since my last kill, and there were pieces of myself quite literally beginning to slough away. If I didn't find something to sink my dagger into soon, I would no longer possess the strength, and after that… Well, it didn't matter, because from the looks of Cedric, he needed a solution within the same timeframe.

And if one of us was going to die, it sure as fuck wasn't going to be him.

I was only vaguely aware of Scarlett saying my name and didn't fully emerge from my thoughts until Cedric said it too. Only he didn't call me Elvira, as he would have in any other circumstance. He uttered my childhood nickname, trying yet failing to conceal the pain from his voice. "I'll be fine, Elle. Just patch me up like you always do. I'll keep still this time, I pro… What are you doing?"

Hearing 'Elle' triggered something in me, something far beyond the rot and desperation currently threatening to eat me alive. If my brother was calling me that, he was the furthest thing from fine, and I wouldn't know a moment's peace until he was once again healed and whole. Ignoring both Cedric and Scarlett, I began rifling through the desk and documents with reckless abandon, searching for the list of plants and their uses we'd been compiling over the time we'd been imprisoned here. The chances of an herbal remedy undoing the damage of a lethal infection were beyond slim, if not impossible, but without any way to leave Neverland and go into town for proper, stronger medicine—the curse kept us trapped here—it was Cedric's one and only chance of recovery.

"Damn it, where is it?" I hissed, carelessly shoving aside a stack of old maps detailing lands far beyond this one; it wasn't as if we would need them again, anyway. "Where is that list of flora I *told* you to keep safe?"

"Careful!" Cedric made a feeble attempt to reach for me, wincing as he no doubt aggravated his wound. "Those are my—"

"Obsessive scribblings about undead children? Yeah, I've gathered as much." I wasn't taking a careful look at the papers beyond ensuring they weren't what I needed, but on each of the ones Cedric had touched in recent weeks, the name 'Peter Pan' was written on them all at least once.

"Immortal children," he grumbled, but I'd stopped listening to yank open another drawer, this time discovering something I'd long since forgotten: a music box.

I'd hardly done any more than reach for it before something shoved me away with force, and the next thing I knew, Scarlett had the tarnished old thing tucked protectively beneath her elbow. We locked eyes, but she didn't offer an apology or explanation as she shuffled away with the music box in tow, and I knew better than to ask for one. For whatever reason, she'd always been fond of the old thing, and I was more than happy to leave her to it. At least now I was free to rifle through Cedric's drawers as chaotically as I liked, which is precisely what I did for the next several minutes. Books, letters, charts, and journals alike were all tossed aside, and had my brother not been in such a state, I'd have given him an earful for the disorganized and downright disgraceful state of his desk.

Right as I began to suspect Cedric may have used the parchment as fodder for more of his nonsensical fixation on Peter and his band of boys, I found it. Tucked away beneath a pile of maps and charts was the list of Neverland's plant life I'd worked so hard to compile during our first few weeks here; a list that now might just save my brother's life. I grabbed it and immediately began scanning the page for any possible cure that might help him. There were dozens of listings—some familiar, like the ones I'd used to concoct my poisons, and others whose properties I'd yet to discover—but none seemed to offer any hope. Panic began to set in as I read over each plant again and again, desperately searching for something, anything, that could help Cedric. But among the list of known plants, there was nothing, at least nothing certain; anything I used on him would be experimental at best and could kill him at worst. I was desperate enough to gamble, yes, but certainly not when it came to my brother's life.

Scarlett either sensed my despair or saw it on my face, and as she leaned in, her harrowing whisper was uttered for my ears alone. "He needs medicine, Elvira."

"And where do you suggest we get any?" I hissed, only barely fighting back tears. "All we have to work with is what's right here."

"But what if there's a way out?"

I stilled at that. My voice was already low, but I dropped it even further as I met Scarlett's gaze. "Are you saying you've found one?"

"No," she said quickly, casting a glance in Cedric's direction. "But I *am* suggesting that's where our efforts might be better spent. Getting out of here. Surely there's something we haven't tried."

I shook my head before she'd even finished. "That's yet another unknown. Even if it were possible, how do you know the curse wouldn't strike us dead the moment we set foot back in the outside world? What if—"

"No one is going anywhere," Cedric cut across me then, and Scarlett and I both looked up to find him scowling at us. "And that's an order, because last I checked, I'm still your captain. Elvira, patch me up, and patch me up *now*. I need to…" His voice trailed off as the little color remaining in his face vanished, and he blinked rapidly, as if struggling to keep us in focus. "I need…"

Sensing what was about to happen a moment before it did, I rushed over, only barely managing to catch Cedric as he tumbled from his chair. Scarlett was at my side a moment later, but we didn't place him back where he'd been. We dragged him to his bed, laying him stomach down so I still had access to his wound.

Scarlett took one look at it before covering her mouth and

gagging, quickly averting her gaze. "Elvira, this is *bad*."

"Hand me my supplies." I refused to fully register her words and climbed on Cedric's bed with him, positioning myself atop the small of his back. He twitched but didn't otherwise react to me or my weight, and I wasn't certain if that was a good or bad thing. Turning back to Scarlett, who had returned with what was left of the rum and dressings, I took it and said, "Hold him."

She swallowed. "What?"

"I need you to hold his shoulders," I snapped, harsher now. "Do you want him to live, or not?"

Scarlett hesitated for a moment then reached out and tentatively placed her hands where I'd indicated. Cedric reacted immediately and violently to her touch, but even as she held firm, Scarlett's expression was nearly as tortured as Cedric's had been mere minutes ago. Watching them and what their relationship had become stirred something within me, but just as I had done with anything resembling an emotion, I forced myself to shove it aside.

I quickly got to work cleaning the wound, using what was hopefully a clean cloth and the remnants of the rum. Cedric's body tensed with each touch, and he let out a muffled groan as I dabbed at it. Scarlett continued to hold him in place, her grip tightening with each passing second. Tears brimmed in her eyes, and she looked away, but still she held on, doing her best to keep Cedric still while I worked.

It was difficult to tell if I had even done anything, but once satisfied that the wound was as clean as it was going to get, I began applying ointment and dressing it up with bandages. It was a slow process, made all the more difficult by Cedric's constant writhing. Every time my hand moved too close or touched something particularly tender on his skin, he would cry out and try to pull away from our grip. Despite his attempts to break free, I was able to finish wrapping up his wound relatively quickly.

Finally finished, Scarlett and I stepped back, taking a moment to catch our breath as Cedric slipped into a fitful sleep. He continued to twitch and mumble nonsense, and more than once I was tempted to get up and wipe the sweat from his brow and back, but something kept me rooted in place as a single word seared itself into my mind: *temporary*. Anything less than a cure for the infection ravaging Cedric's body would do nothing more than temporarily ease his pain, temporarily extend his life, and he needed far more than temporary.

"I take it back," Scarlett finally said, pulling me from my thoughts. "It's not medicine that he needs. It's a fucking miracle."

Balling my hands into fists, it took everything I had not to whirl around and punch her. "I'm getting incredibly tired of you stating the obvious without offering any tangible solutions."

"I *did* offer one. It's hardly my fault you weren't willing to hear it."

"Because it wasn't a solution, it was certain death. Or at the very least"—I gestured to Cedric—"his death. We can't waste our time on 'what ifs,' Scarlett. We just can't."

"We can't?" she asked quietly, meeting my gaze. Though there was no challenge in her voice, there was an unmistakable one in her eyes. "Or *you* can't?"

Her words turned my blood to ice for more reasons than one. I studied her closely, searching for any hint of what I'd clearly missed.

"When did you stop loving him?"

Scarlett's mouth fell open. "When the hell did I say that?"

"You didn't have to. Not when you don't want to be anywhere near him, let alone touch him, you're more than willing to gamble with his life, and you're clearly running from something given how hellbent you are on getting out of here. So the question remains: when did you stop loving him?"

She shook her head before I'd finished speaking, and wetness glistened in her eyes. "It's not that simple, and was never a question of love. It's that sometimes, love alone isn't enough."

"Not enough for what, to keep you here? To care whether he lives or dies?"

"For Adais's sake, of course I care!"

"Do you? Because even if you did manage to find a way out, I'm not fully convinced you'd return."

Scarlett's lips pressed into a thin line, her gaze never leaving mine. "Careful, Elvira. You don't know what you're talking about."

"I very much do," I said, my voice low and steady. "You want out, and Cedric's incapacitated state is a rather convenient excuse for you to do just that."

"That isn't true!" she hissed, visibly trembling with rage. "And if only you knew…"

"Knew what?" I pressed when Scarlett's voice trailed off.

"Nothing," she finally said, and in an instant, her emotional display was replaced with a stony façade, one even I knew better than to attempt to penetrate.

But it didn't prevent me from having a reaction regardless. My fists tightened as red-hot fury coursed through me, but for once, I didn't know what to say. How could I when I'd thought this day would never come? I hardly believed in love, and even less in soulmates, but if the latter existed, Cedric and Scarlett were it. I hadn't witnessed the birth of their relationship, but I'd seen more than enough of it to be unable to imagine a reality in which they weren't together. They'd squabbled over the years and had even fought far worse than this more times than I could count. So what was so different about this fight?

And what was Scarlett not telling me?

We stared at each other for a few moments before I finally stepped away, shaking my head in defeat. Both my and Cedric's clocks were ticking—mine because of my rot, his because of his infection—and I didn't have a moment left to waste arguing in circles or attempting to pry information out of Scarlett she clearly wasn't going to offer freely. "Fine," I said flatly. "If you won't help, I'll find someone who will."

After snatching the list of flora from Cedric's desk, I located my jacket and donned it as I headed for the door. I'd anticipated Scarlett to protest and had braced myself to ignore it, but what I didn't anticipate was her darting in front of the door, barring the only exit.

"Wait. Does that mean you'll try, after all?" Something glimmered in her eyes…hope? "You mean to leave, to seek someone outside Neverland?"

"I seek what's *certain*. There are other people inhabiting this forest, and one of them has got to know how to help my brother. The immortal children, perhaps, or maybe even—"

"The natives?" Scarlett's eyes nearly popped out of her head. "You can't be serious. If there are any left, they'll kill you on sight."

So be it, I bit back just in time. "They may be our only hope. *Cedric's* only hope. They've been here for generations and surely have a remedy for infections or can at least direct me to the plants I'd need to make my own. Now move."

Scarlett stood firm even when I shoved her with all my might, which admittedly wasn't much given my weakened state. "How is this any less foolish than my plan? This is suicide, and you know it."

"Maybe, and maybe not. But I have to try, and you cannot stop me."

She stared at me for a long while before dipping her head in defeat, exhaling through her teeth. "In that case, I'm coming with—"

"No!" I practically shouted before casting a glance in Cedric's direction to make certain I hadn't woken him. When I was sure I hadn't, I lowered my voice and said, "He can't afford to lose us both, and especially not you. You know that. Besides, he needs at least one of us to stand guard and keep bringing him rats."

Scarlett looked as though I'd stabbed her. "But you… You can't…"

"Can't what, save my brother's ass?" I laughed darkly. "It's not as if I'm not used to it. Been doing it nearly since he took his first breaths."

Though she still looked very much like she wanted to argue, Scarlett finally conceded, stepping away from the door just enough for me to yank it open and slip by. Before I closed it, her voice rang out a final time.

"Be careful, Elvira, and please come back. Cedric needs you."

I vehemently disagreed.

I'd save Cedric, or I would die trying, because there was no doubt in my mind that my brother would survive losing me.

But I wouldn't survive losing him.

II. THE SWALLOW

The rot had spread.

Tugging up the sleeve of my tattered shirt, I grimaced at the blackening veins snaking down my right arm. I'd last dared to look around midday, when the decay still hovered above my elbow. It was nearly dusk now, and in that short time, it had both passed that point and reached several inches beyond. If I didn't kill tonight, no doubt it would reach my fingertips by morning, and once that happened… I didn't know, because never before had I allowed it to get this bad, and I'd been cursed well before Cedric had accidentally spread it to all the inhabitants of Neverland. Would the entire limb turn black? Would I still be able to use it? I could barely use it now and had to grit my teeth even to flex my palm. The pain couldn't get any worse, surely, because the next stage was losing sensation entirely.

Silver linings, I supposed.

With a snort, I trudged onward through the dense forest, swatting away gnats and mosquitoes with my good hand as my boots squelched in the mud with every step. The canopy overhead was so thick barely any sunlight filtered through. An unnatural chill hung in the air, as if all the life below had been replaced by death, and given the curse, indeed it had. I'd barely gotten a chance to know Neverland prior to the rot and decay ravaging it, but I still vaguely recalled how it had once been teeming with life. The assortment of creatures this forest inhabited included many I'd never seen before—fairies, sirens, mermaids, and direwolves to name just a few, and there had to be dozens more.

But thanks to my other brother, Jamie, all that was long gone now. In his greed for their dust, he'd hunted the fairies to extinction, his curse had turned the direwolves into what we now called Nightstalkers, and the mermaids and sirens had begun breeding with one another, creating vicious and bloodthirsty monstrosities known as nerisas. The humans of Neverland had fared no better. Peter Pan had lost several of his boys thanks to various members of our crew needing a kill, and as for the natives, no one had glimpsed any of them for close to two months now. Whispers that they had either hunted themselves to extinction or we had done it for them had begun to spread, and the pessimistic part of me believed them.

If even a single one had lived, though, I was more than determined to seek them out. Thanks to Cedric's idiotic feud with Peter, the boy and his band would be of no use, especially once they learned my goal was to save the life of their mortal enemy, so the natives were my only hope. We knew next to nothing about them, other than they were a highly elusive and adaptable people who had inhabited this land for generations. They may not possess modern weaponry such as guns or cannons, but not only were they skilled archers and trappers, they knew this land, and they knew it well.

So they *had* to know about healing infections. They simply had to. And if I kept walking, heading deeper into unknown territory than I'd ever gone before, I'd happen upon one sooner or later. And once I did, all I had to do was convince them to spill whatever secrets they knew… and not to kill me.

I'm so fucked.

As much as I was loath to admit it, the longer I walked, the more convinced I became that Scarlett was right: this *was* asinine, far more than her idea of trying to find a way out of Neverland. But what choice did I have, especially when we'd attempted as much and failed spectacularly every time? Ever since the curse had taken hold, leaving the forest had been impossible for every pirate who'd tried. It wasn't that we didn't know the way out. It was that any time anyone headed in the direction of Afterport, the town that bordered Neverland, the trees kept changing, always guiding you right back to where you started rather than out. Turning to the beaches was no better. Anyone who attempted to swim away had been carried back to shore by a rogue wave if they were lucky, and bashed against the rocks or drowned if they weren't.

"I'm so fucked," I muttered, aloud this time, because the truth of it was that no matter what, Cedric's chances of survival were slim at best, and nonexistent at worst. I'd die before admitting it, but part of the reason I'd gotten so angry with Scarlett was because she'd seemed so detached over the whole scenario, so far removed from the fact that her lover was wasting away before her eyes. If Cedric truly was going to die, I desperately wished I could be like Scarlett: guard my heart by locking it far, far away from the hurt that would inevitably wound it beyond repair. But with him especially, I'd never been able to do such a thing. Cedric may be the biggest pain in the ass I'd ever had the misfortune to know, but he was my brother, and I loved him almost more fiercely than I loathed him.

Almost.

I continued on for the rest of the day and through most of the night without rest, not stopping even when I lost all sensation in my right arm as the rot finally overtook it. My left was still mostly intact—for now—my legs had yet to give out, and a Nightstalker had yet to devour me, so perhaps the gods were smiling upon me after all. A bitter laugh escaped my lips. I didn't bother to stifle it given that I'd long since ceased any attempts to be quiet. After all, I *wanted* to be found. "And Adais willing, let it be soon."

Nearly the same moment the scathing whisper left my lips, a foul stench assaulted my nostrils, vile even for Neverland's standards. I gagged, raising my good hand over my mouth and nose as I took in what was just ahead. A large pile of corpses lay in a clearing, with most already rotted down to bone. Maggots writhed in the hollows of eye sockets and open mouths, eating away at the remaining flesh and sinew, while a handful of crows squabbled over the best places to sit and feast. The bodies were so decayed that they would have been unidentifiable if not for the antlers, because only one of Neverland's creatures sported them.

Nightstalkers, then, but that wasn't what worried me; what did is what had killed them. The beasts were well known to kill their own kind, of course, but this wasn't a squabble over food, territory, or simply a need to stave off their own curse. This was a massacre, and the only beings capable of slaughtering Nightstalkers on this scale were—

My head whipped in the direction of where a twig had snapped. It was a miracle I'd heard it given how dulled my senses were in my weakened state, but the moment I caught sight of an eerie, almost ethereal blue glow was the same moment I realized the sound had been intentional.

Half shrouded by the trees stood the unmistakable silhouette of a woman. The distance between us, as well as her dark braided hair, hid most of details of her face, but the sharpness of her gaze was accentuated by the luminescent paint with which she'd marked her cheeks and forehead. Her clothes were simple by contrast— undecorated leathers—and the one adornment she'd allowed herself was a blue feather woven into her braids. She carried a bow, and the quiver at her back was well stocked with arrows whose feathers matched the one in her hair, but most curious of all was the fact that she didn't move a muscle as we stared at one another: Neverlander and pirate, native and intruder, and given our current circumstances, predator and prey.

What the hell was she waiting for?

She'd made the sound on purpose—of that, I was certain. I was equally certain she'd been the one to kill all these Nightstalkers. Was this how she'd done it? Made her presence known before taunting the beasts to rush her? But if that were the case, surely the corpses would be littered with arrows, and I hadn't glimpsed a single one nestled within the pile of bodies.

So there must be something else. A trap, perhaps, one she hoped to lead me into. But why not shoot me and be done with it? I was more than close enough for her to land a fatal shot if her aim was as decent as I suspected, and if not, surely she was at least capable of wounding me. Was it up to me to make the first move? Would she even react?

My body decided before my mind could say otherwise and took the smallest of steps forward. I tensed, bracing for the arrow that was surely about to pierce my breast, but when nothing came, I raised my gaze to hers once more. Other than the slightest twitch of her brow, she remained as still and silent as ever. So still I wondered whether she'd be there if I dared to blink.

She was.

Not an illusion, then, but that wasn't the part I was having a difficult time believing. The longer I remained alive, the more rage began to fester within me. Was she really such an efficient killer that she had no need to take my life to sate her own curse? Or did she find me unworthy of even putting forth the effort to do so? Was I truly no better than a beast, one who would have no doubt rushed to its own death by now?

There wasn't time to untangle the complicated reasoning surrounding my current emotions. I didn't want to die—I *had* to live, if only to save Cedric—and it was high time I made that clear to this stranger who, for whatever reason, didn't want to kill me, either… for now.

Before I lost my nerve, I reached into my pocket, pulling out the list of flora. She didn't move a muscle as I unfolded it, nor when I held it up for her to see. "Plants," I explained, managing to raise my rotten arm just enough to point to several bushes and trees scattered around us before gesturing back to the list. "I need to know which plants are good for infections."

Her gaze narrowed, but given that she didn't reach for her bow, I hurriedly continued, "Please. It's for my brother. He's very sick and needs help quickly."

Dread knotted in my stomach as I spoke, and the urge to scream became nearly overwhelming. Not because I wasn't being heard, but because only now was it clear just how much my desperation had clouded my judgment. Here I stood, alone, dehydrated, and so weak I could barely stand, pleading with a woman who likely couldn't understand a word I was saying.

This was hopeless. Cedric was going to die and so was I, either by this woman's hand or by the rot consuming me completely. Had it finally begun eating away at my mind, and that was yet another reason I wasn't thinking straight? If that was truly the case, I'd sooner end it myself.

After crumpling the list and shoving it back in my pocket, I drew one of the daggers strapped to my left side. I'd barely raised it before the woman responded, lifting her bow and nocking an arrow in a fluid, graceful motion, and only then did I realize she'd misunderstood my intention. Even at full draw, she held her weapon steady and still, her expression as cold and impassive as before. The corner of her lips twitched, almost as if playing at a smirk… or perhaps a scowl. Had I surprised her? Pissed her off? Good, honestly. Perhaps I didn't need to end it when she looked more than happy to do the honors for me.

But yet again, nothing came.

"What the devil are you waiting for?" I shouted this time, allowing the dagger to slip from my grip as I raised my good arm in surrender. Despite the circumstances, I laughed, and the sound of it was as bitter as the taste in my mouth. "I'm right here, and the easiest shot you'll ever have."

I flinched when she spoke, but only because I hadn't been expecting her to. Her response was low and terse, spoken in a language I didn't understand, but whatever she'd said didn't concern me nearly as much as the fact that her eyes had widened.

Was she trying to warn me? And if so, of what?

Before I made sense of any of it, several things happened at once.

Muffled shouts sounded from the trees behind me, but the

moment I whirled around to face them, there came a sharp pain in the back of my upper thigh. Reaching down, I yanked out what had pierced through both clothes and skin, rolling it around in my fingers: a small feathered dart, its barbed tip dripping with both luminescent fluid that perfectly matched the woman's facial paint and now, my own blood. Irritation replaced my confusion; she'd refused to shoot me, but she'd dart me?

"You… you d-drugged…"

I didn't finish my sentence before arms snaked beneath my elbows, keeping me upright even as my knees buckled beneath me. Though I willed my eyes to blink, darkness clouded my vision instead. More screams soon joined the raucous chorus, piercing the inside of my skull as if a thousand tiny darts had been trapped inside, and I didn't bother to fight as the blackness swallowed me whole.

III. THE CAPTIVE

Everything hurt.

My wrists seared as though they were on fire, my head throbbed at an agonizing, irregular rhythm, and something clawed incessantly at my insides—the rot, no doubt. It took enormous effort to open my eyes, but I groaned and immediately closed them when harsh sunlight assaulted my vision. Daylight, then. But where was I? The vaguest of noises drifted from somewhere nearby, but I was still too dazed to make anything resembling sense of it.

I remained where I was curled up on what felt like dirt, laid completely still, and waited, either for my senses to come back, my memories to catch up, or both. The last thing I remembered was my long, arduous journey, and then coming across the pile of Nightstalker corpses… but then what? And how had I gotten here?

Color flashed in my mind's eye, that bright, bioluminescent blue, followed by a face: *her* face, the woman with the feather in her hair. I'd shown her the list of flora but hadn't gotten a response, and then she'd darted me, which must have been how—

The list. Where was it?

Pain exploded from somewhere in my chest as I miraculously managed to push myself upright, but my panic overshadowed most of it. Only when I shoved my aching hands into my pockets did I realize my wrists had been bound together in front of me, yet even that was little deterrent as I dug deeper and more furiously, fingers clawing at what soon proved to be just empty fabric. They'd taken it, then—the one thing I might have been able to use to communicate with people who didn't speak any of the languages I did—and the final hope I had for saving Cedric's life.

I felt for my daggers next, and it was far less of a shock to find that those had been taken, too. If my bound wrists weren't enough of an indication that I was a prisoner, my lack of weapons certainly was, as were the wooden stakes surrounding me on all sides. It took a few more moments of staring before I put together that the stakes were a cage, and an effective one at that. When I crawled forward and yanked at the nearest one, it didn't have the slightest bit of give. There was space between them, yes, but not nearly enough for me to slip through.

My thoughts raced as fear finally took root in my mind. For myself but mostly for Cedric. Was he safe? Was he *alive*? Had Scarlett managed to keep herself together in my absence, or had she, too, fallen prey to her fears? It had been nearly two days since I'd left them. Did they believe I'd return? Or had they already given up hoping?

The list of questions tumbling endlessly through my mind only grew longer as the haze dulling my senses subsided a bit, which proved to be a blessing and a curse. I could hear better now, and my ears immediately informed me that the sound I'd heard upon waking was in fact human voices, but I could smell better, too, and the putrid filth and decay that assaulted my nostrils nearly made me vomit on the spot. Forcing myself to swallow the bile that had risen in my throat, I turned my gaze to where half a dozen figures stood crowded around one another, arguing in the same language I'd heard the woman who had darted me speak earlier. Though I couldn't comprehend a word, the subject of their heated discussion was more than clear given the frequent glances and gestures in my direction.

I should have moved back, or at the very least not have gaped at the captors currently deciding my fate. Hell, I should have been worried *about* said fate, especially one that would prevent me from returning to Cedric. But all I could do was stare wide-eyed at them and our surroundings, as mesmerized as I was impressed by all of it. These people, the natives of Neverland, were not only alive, but thriving, at least compared to how we pirates were faring. My prison looked to be near the outskirts of their village, but even through the bars of my cage, I could make out a camp teeming with life. Mothers watched over their children, elders sat around a smokeless fire, and a group of warriors, men and women alike, were tending to their various weapons—sharpening spear heads, crafting arrows, and re-stringing bows. A few even fiddled with what looked to be intricate, handcrafted traps. Most curious, though, was that all of them, no matter their age or rank, were marked with luminescent paint in some way. While the majority of them didn't wear it on their face—that seemed to be a distinction reserved solely for the warriors—the rest sported it somewhere on their arms or shoulders. What was its purpose, I wondered, and what made it so important that they all wore it? Was it simply part of their culture, or was there another reason?

Though my knees screamed in protest, I propped myself up on them to get a closer look, failing to notice the figure who had approached my cage until it was too late. I flinched and shuffled back when a spear was thrust into the dirt mere inches from where I sat, and not simply because the force of it striking the ground had splattered mud onto my face. A man came into view a moment later, a warrior, judging from the intricate markings on his face and the numerous weapons strapped in various places along his well-muscled body. His lips curled into a sneer as he knelt to my level, and he barked out a laugh that sent chills down my spine as he took in my no doubt animalistic appearance as I huddled, bound and shivering, at the back of my cage.

Was that what I was to them—an animal they'd hunted for

sport? Prey to be slaughtered at the appropriate moment? It made far more sense than I wanted to admit. If the woman who'd found me wasn't in need of a kill to sate her curse, surely someone else in this village was, or would be soon. And that meant the question wasn't *if* they were going to kill me. The question was when.

It was only when the man spoke that my fear gave way to rage. These people may have drugged, captured, and bound me, but they hadn't killed me yet, and I sure as fuck didn't plan on making it easy for them, especially not while Cedric still needed me. So when the man spoke again, louder this time, I surged forward, slamming myself against the bars of the cage before gripping and shaking them, if only to hide my own uncontrollable quivering. A voice whispered in my ear, one that sounded suspiciously like Cedric's: *Show no weakness. Show no fear.*

I didn't plan to.

"If you're going to kill me, you'd best get on with it," I spat with as much venom as I could muster. My face was mere inches from the warrior's, and I hope he'd noticed that I'd filed several of my teeth into sharp points. I hoped even more that I'd get an opportunity to sink them into his flesh. "Because if you let me sit here and fester, I promise you, I *will* get out of here, and when I do, I won't hesitate to—"

I had expected the warrior to react in some way. What I *hadn't* expected was for yet another shape to come hurtling toward us. Even the warrior was caught off guard as the newcomer shoved him with so much force he was thrown off balance, and if he hadn't been able to grab his spear for support, no doubt he'd have crumpled to the unforgiving ground.

Raising my gaze, I inhaled sharply when I took in the sight of yet another warrior: the woman from the forest. The feather in her hair quivered with her obvious anger as she began shouting at her comrade, waving her arms as she pointed first to me, and then to the general direction of their village. Though I probably should have, I didn't bother to speculate the specifics of what they might be discussing. Instead, I watched the exchange, mirroring the same mixture of awe and fear the warrior with the spear was no doubt feeling. The woman was much shorter and slimmer in stature than him, but he bowed his head as she spoke and only dared to mumble a curt reply once she'd finished. With a snort and jerk of her chin, she dismissed him, and once the warrior had scrambled away, it left only her and me. My heart began to flutter as she eyed me up and down, this time from anticipation rather than fear. Was I finally about to get some answers?

But she didn't say a word. She just stared, long and hard, and though a million questions hovered at the tip of my tongue, I found myself unable to do anything but stare right back. Now that she stood out in the open rather than in the shadows of the forest, I got my first real look at her. Physically, she appeared to be right around my age, but given that time worked so differently in Neverland, it was impossible to know how old she actually was. Her eyes were as dark as her hair, and both were illuminated by the blueish-green glow of her luminescent paint. She carried no weapons other than a single dagger sheathed at her left hip, so she must have left her bow and quiver somewhere else. Of all things, though, my gaze kept flicking back to the swallow's feather hovering just in front of her right ear. The feather itself wasn't remarkable, but at least so far she was the only native I'd glimpsed wearing one.

I wasn't certain how long we gaped at one another, but the moment our eyes locked was the moment she spun on her heel and stalked away. Panic surged in my chest, but there was no time to wonder why I suddenly craved the company of this woman. She'd shielded me from the other warrior, yes, but for all I knew it was simply because she planned on killing me herself the moment she needed one to sate her curse. She had been the one to stumble upon me, so perhaps that meant she, and she alone, was entitled to take my life.

"Wait," I rasped through parched and cracked lips, gripping the bars of my cage until my knuckles turned white. "Can you understand me? ¿Puedes entenderme? What's going to happen to me? ¿Lo que me va a pasar? You can't just leave me here!"

I screamed until my throat was raw, alternating between English and Spanish, but not only did my cries fall upon deaf ears, the woman with the feather in her hair didn't reappear for the rest of the afternoon.

The day passed both quickly and agonizingly slowly. Once it became abundantly clear I was going to be ignored, I refocused my energy on surviving my pain, which was rapidly becoming as unbearable as it was unsustainable. I'd been bluffing earlier when the warrior had taunted me. I barely possessed the energy to lift my head let alone enact revenge on the people who'd taken me prisoner and kept me from my brother, and unless and until I got a kill, I'd be useless.

Eventually, the sun dipped below the horizon, casting eerie shadows across the camp. The Natives' voices dissipated into a hushed silence, as if the world itself was holding its breath, and in a way it was, given what prowled Neverland's forests after dark. Leaning against the cold bars of my cage as the nighttime chill seeped through my tattered clothing and into my bones, the sudden quiet only amplified my thoughts. Though my own future was yet to be decided, it was Cedric who occupied my every worry. My imagination twisted, conjuring horrific images of him writhing and screaming in pain, the infection spreading with each passing moment, all while I was powerless to stop it.

Despite my mental anguish, as the darkness deepened, exhaustion claimed me, and I found myself drifting in and out of sleep. Dreams laced with dread flooded my mind, as did Cedric's cries, yet given that sleep was the sole reprieve from the pounding ache in my wrists and the rot eating away at any part of me it hadn't yet touched, I gladly gave in.

At some point, I jolted awake, heart thudding against my chest. I thought the lingering threads of a nightmare had roused me, but when I turned my head toward the faintest traces of light, I did a double take before nearly leaping out of my skin.

The woman with the feather sat cross-legged just outside

my cage. Paint shimmering against her warm sepia skin was the light I'd glimpsed, and in near darkness, the markings made her look almost otherworldly. She didn't move or speak even when a groan of pain escaped my lips as I switched positions, so I took the opportunity to scan our immediate surroundings. From the looks of it, we were alone.

"What are you doing here?" The words left my lips cautiously, barely more than a whisper. She didn't respond, fixing her dark eyes on me with an unreadable expression as she drew her lips into a thin line. "Why am *I* here?" I dared to press. "Better yet, why am I still alive?"

Silence stretched between us, but maddening as it was, it no longer felt entirely useless. With no other method of communication available to us, these stretches of quiet were all we had with which to build some sort of bridge, and for now, at least, it was within my best interests to embrace them.

I couldn't let them go on for too long though, because that's when the nightmares began to creep back in. So I began to ramble, blurting out whatever thoughts came to mind in that same hushed whisper. "Given that you can't understand a word I'm saying, I may as well admit it. I think you're quite pretty. Beautiful, even."

Unless I'd imagined it, her hardened expression softened ever so slightly, but I'd more readily believe that my addled mind was simply clinging to whatever hope it could.

"It's because you stand out, compared to the rest of your people, mostly because of that feather in your hair. Speaking of which—your people, not the feather—do they know you're out here?" I searched her face intently. "What do they plan to do with me?"

More silence, but she did lift her chin ever so slightly. An unnerving chill swept through the cage, and I hugged myself tighter, trying in vain to retain some semblance of warmth. "You must have some idea, anything at all. I'm not asking because I'm trying to prevent it. I'm sure you can tell I'm far too weak for that. I just want to know what's coming, to better prepare for the inevitable."

There was no answer save for the wind rustling through the treetops above.

"Fine," I snapped, gritting my teeth in frustration. "If you won't tell me what it is you're planning, tell me about yourself. What is your name? Why do you wear that feather?" She'd seemed to appreciate my earlier compliment despite not fully understanding it, so with any luck, my sincere curiosity would shine through enough to add to whatever bridge we had begun to build. "It's pretty, too. Bonita."

Something flickered in her eyes. Interest, perhaps? She offered no response though, leaving me to yet again wonder if I had misinterpreted it or was simply seeing things.

Still, I was oddly enjoying this one-sided conversation; it was nice to talk to someone who wasn't a pirate about something other than Cedric. "Does the feather mark you as someone of authority? Is that why the other warrior listened to you earlier?"

My words ricocheted off the walls of her silence, and each unanswered question only added to my mounting frustration. But despite her apparent unwillingness to engage with me, she seemed to be listening, taking in my every word. She continued to take in *me* as well, scanning me up and down as if she intended to memorize every inch of me.

I bit my lip, shrinking beneath the weight of her gaze as it bore into mine. The longer we sat here, the more charged the air between us felt, and the more invasive—and intimate—each of her looks became. If anyone else had sat here gawking at me like an exhibit on display for even half as long, I wouldn't have allowed it, much less… enjoyed it.

Swallowing hard, I blurted out more questions before I could examine that revelation too deeply. "Why did you spare me yesterday? Why am I here instead of my corpse added to that pile of dead Nightstalkers?"

The intensity of her stare never wavered, but I could have sworn yet another shadow flickered across her face. But like all the others, it disappeared as quickly as it came, and her infuriating silence remained unbroken.

"Please," I whispered, shocking even myself with my words. Never in my life had I begged anyone for anything, but my need to know why she'd spared me had grown nearly as desperate as my need to save Cedric's life. "If you tell me nothing else, tell me why I'm still alive."

Her silence stretched on, as heavy and suffocating as the humid Neverland air, and with a groan, I finally sat back. My chest rose and fell in a haggard rhythm, and only now that I'd shifted positions did I realize how difficult it had become to breathe. I'd been saying it for days, but it seemed my body truly meant it now. There wasn't much time left before this curse and its rot claimed me.

A dark laugh escaped me; my peripheral vision told me she was still there. "Is this why you haven't killed me? So you can watch me die?"

The smallest of noises escaped her then, and I whipped my head in her direction just in time to see her avert her gaze, as though she couldn't bear to acknowledge the truth of my words. But when she turned back to face me, that guarded expression was back once more, leaving me no clues as to what that noise may have been about. And still, she said nothing.

"Fine," I spat again, truly angry now. "Have your little show. I hope it's a good one."

Shifting until my back was to her, I curled into myself, more to hide the tears that had begun streaming down my cheeks rather than because I couldn't stand to look at her anymore, because I very much could. Much as she infuriated and confused me, I meant what I'd said earlier. She was beautiful, perhaps the most beautiful thing in Neverland, and if these truly were my final days, I could have far worse things to look at.

Sound pulled me from my thoughts—footsteps—but by the time I'd rolled my half-rotten body back over, she was gone.

Dread constricted my throat, and once again I couldn't breathe, this time for an entirely different reason. "Wait!" I called after her as loud as I dared, but my cries died in the night air, swallowed by both the silence and the shadows. Even still, I kept pleading for her to come back, as unwilling to be alone as I was to admit that I needed or even wanted her.

But I silenced abruptly when, from not very far away, a scream rang out. Given that Nightstalker screams sounded unnervingly similar to a human's, there was no way to tell which of them it might be. I froze as my blood turned to ice, straining to hear any other sounds… but there was nothing. Not even a whisper.

I was no stranger to the horrors of Neverland. I'd already lost one brother to them, and a second was well on his way. The monsters were bad enough on their own, but time and time again, they proved far less of a threat than the monsters the curse turned each of us into. It made us as desperate as we were bloodthirsty, and as I was currently learning the hard way, there was no escape from any of it.

Huddling at the back corner of my cage, I clutched the bars for support when the sounds of the forest returned, each faraway roar and snarl taunting as much as it mocked me. Somewhere out there, death was on the hunt. And I feared with every fiber of my being that once it claimed Cedric, its gaze would turn next to me.

IV. THE RAT

I wished more than anything I was dead.

If what I'd felt yesterday had been pain, the sensations currently running through what was left of my body were nothing short of torture. It hurt to blink, it hurt to breathe, and my own blood felt like poison—from the looks of it, it was. Blackened veins trickled down my arms and legs, circulating liquid death from my heart to my extremities and back again. The sight rather reminded me of Cedric and his infected wound, and no doubt I was now feeling every bit of what he must have felt, only amplified tenfold.

I could no longer move, could no longer think unless it was about the pain, but I could and did scream. Sometimes my lips formed words, sometimes they didn't, but no matter what came out fell upon deaf ears. The natives went about their daily lives, content to pretend I simply wasn't there, and of course there was no sign of the warrior with the feather. Perhaps it was for the best, given that I no longer knew what it was I wanted. A swift death, yes, but even in this state, there was still part of me convinced that I'd somehow be able to make it out of this mess and save Cedric. All I needed was a single kill, and anything living would do. A rat, a fish, even a damn beetle could be my salvation. But it wouldn't bring satisfaction, and that was what I craved more than anything—to sate the bloodlust of my mind rather than just my body, and I'd fixated on one target in particular.

Her.

Fantasizing about jamming a knife between the feathered woman's ribs was the only thing that kept me going, especially after several children began kicking my near-lifeless form through the stakes making up my cage. The blows were little more than gentle shoves compared to the agony of the rot, but it was humiliating nonetheless, and despite willing them not to, hot tears began rolling down my cheeks as a single word began repeating endlessly in my mind: pathetic. It was what I'd become, no matter how badly I wanted to deny it.

Much like 'weak' and 'useless', I'd run from the term all my life. Anyone who had the misfortune to have any such label assigned to them didn't last long among Father's crew or aboard the *Queen Anne's Revenge*, and my sex alone meant that fate was far more likely for me than it was for any man. I'd had to train twice as hard, be twice as strong, and infinitely more cunning to even compare to my older brothers, and even then, I couldn't become complacent for even a second. It would be a lie to say that I didn't enjoy killing and plundering—I very much did—but even still, it would have been nice to have more of a choice in the direction of my own life.

I supposed that was why I hated the woman with the feather so much. We may not have exchanged a single word in a language we could both understand, but we didn't have to, not when it was more than clear she was everything I wasn't. Her beauty was an insult, her strength a mockery, and it was obvious from the way she carried herself that her worth had never been tied to being better than her brothers, or anyone for that matter. She may have spared me thus far, but all that had done was prolong my torment and suffering, leaving me to wonder if some sadistic part of her enjoyed watching me writhe in agony. It must be true, given that she nor anyone else came to end me once and for all.

So as the day wore on and my loathing for her festered nearly as much as my rotting body, there was only a single thought capable of bringing me any solace.

She may have hesitated, but I sure as fuck wouldn't, and given half the chance, I'd kill her without a shred of remorse.

At some point, day turned to night… or perhaps my vision was finally going, too. Time dragged by agonizingly slowly, and my strength waned with each passing second. Truthfully, I had no idea how I was still alive. The gods were either pitying or mocking me, and I couldn't decide which was worse. My anguish was unbearable, with the rot gnawing at both my sanity and remaining flesh alike as my breath came in shallow, ragged gasps that were only growing further apart. I wanted to scream, but my tongue had swelled to the point where the only noises I could make now were muffled whimpers. Not long after that, what little sound my ears could pick up began blending together, and I supposed it was only a matter of time before I went deaf as well.

This was it. I was going to die right here in the dirt, rotting, alone, splattered in mud and my own tears, and no one was coming to save me. Given how little the natives seemed to care for me or my existence, I envisioned them leaving my corpse right where it was to finish decomposing, for animals to finish stripping all the flesh and sinew from my bones. Was that it—I was to be bait to attract more Nightstalkers? The cage was positioned far enough away from the main camp that it certainly didn't seem out of the realm of possibility. As if on cue, screams echoed faintly in some faraway part of my psyche, and despite myself, I smiled. The chance was slim, but in my addled state, it was far easier to pretend that the cries were *hers*.

And then… a voice, but I couldn't make out its words. Something pounded against my ribcage that wasn't the rot, and it took me a moment to register that my heartbeat had accelerated in response to whatever I'd heard. Had the gods come to claim me? Was I about to be freed of this torment?

More words, but I didn't bother focusing on them this time, not when my fingertips registered the faintest of sensations. Whatever it was felt cool and smooth against my festering skin. I gripped it with strength that wasn't my own before raising my wrists the slightest bit, slammed them down and then suddenly... relief.

It began slowly at first. Warmth washed over me, wrapping me in a comforting yet familiar embrace before settling deep in my core. As the rot began to recede, drawing back from my limbs like a retreating tide, strength flowed in its place, both filling the void it left behind and purging out the pain. I could hear, I could feel, and I could *move*. My tongue, now back to normal size, darted out to lick my cracked and parched lips, while my fingers and toes twitched of their own accord, eager to get healthy blood flowing into them again. Though it would take time for my body to completely mend itself, especially given my depleted state, in every way, I felt new and whole. But if that were really true, and I wasn't dead, I must have killed, and definitely hadn't done it on my own. And *that* meant—

My eyes flashed open, and there she was, pressed against the stakes that made up my prison and closer to me than she'd ever been. Her lips parted as she watched me push myself into a sitting position, and when she let out the tiniest of sighs, her exhale struck my face. She was still wearing war paint, but had redone it since I'd seen her last. Instead of the pattern I'd become accustomed to, she'd drawn two simple lines which began at her forehead and trailed over each eye before finishing at her chin. The light emitting from the paint wasn't unbearably bright under normal circumstances, but given both the sensitivity of my recovering vision and her close proximity, it forced me to squint a little.

I'd have kept studying her if a weight hadn't lifted from my still bound hands, and glancing down, I realized she'd been holding them. The cool wooden thing I'd gripped had been the hilt of the dagger now back in her possession, and when she pulled her arms away, leaving a clear view of what was underneath, it was my turn to gasp.

Lying lifeless in the dirt was a mangy rat. More blood than I'd have thought possible for its tiny body to possess flowed from the wound in its side and onto the ground below, and a lump formed in my throat. Not at the gruesome sight—at what it meant.

She'd saved me.

A mixture of confusion, relief, and something else flooded through me, but when I turned back to her for answers, she raised a finger to her lips before shaking her head in a clear warning. "No sound," she whispered, and I nodded a split second before registering what had just happened.

Not only had she spoken—she'd spoken in *English*.

Another gasp escaped my lips, both producing an audible squeak and prompting her to scowl. She covered my mouth this time, clamping her fingers firmly over my lips before leaning in until her forehead rested against the stakes that made up my cage.

"I said, be *quiet*. Blink to tell me you understand."

Irritation flared to life within me, and I didn't immediately obey. Was it not obvious that comprehension wasn't the issue? I was far more concerned over the fact that *she spoke English*. And rather than seize any of the multiple opportunities she'd had to speak to me over the past several days, she'd instead allowed me to believe in a nonexistent language barrier.

She'd allowed me to call her pretty.

I blinked quickly, more to conceal the sudden heat rushing to my cheeks than to appease her, and averted my gaze the moment she released me. Never in my life had I felt such raw embarrassment, and yet again I found myself wanting to die—this time for an entirely different reason. Gods, why had I confessed that of all things, and why hadn't I said it in Spanish? For all I knew though, she could secretly speak that language, too, and at this point, such a thing wouldn't surprise me in the least. What else could this woman be hiding, and what were her reasons for hiding it?

"I need to go and get a few things, but I'll be right back." Her voice was low and rough, and her accent sent shivers down my spine, but not because of fear. "And if you make a sound, don't think I won't shoot you."

Apparently threats were attractive, too, because saliva began pooling in my mouth. But I forced myself to nod again, and she slipped into the darkness without another word. For a moment, I remained frozen in place, my skin still tingling in all the places she'd touched me. I did my best to focus on the relief that spread through my body as the rot continued to recede, but as the seconds turned to minutes, that became nearly impossible. My thoughts were consumed by her warm exhales ghosting across my skin, and the unexpected kindness she'd shown me after spending days convinced that this was to be my end.

I glanced at the rat once more before trailing a finger through its bloodied fur, checking whether or not it was real. Warm slickness immediately coated my skin, and though I couldn't make out the color of it in the darkness, it was easy enough to imagine the liquid was crimson. Real, then.

But why?

She had just as many reasons to hate me as I did her. It was impossible to tell which of us had killed more of the other—the pirates or the natives—but even if they had, we were invaders of their territory, and had no claim over this forest or its resources. What's more, *we'd* unleashed the curse, not them, yet they had been just as affected as we were. Perhaps more.

So what the hell was she playing at? If she possessed any sense, any survival instincts at all, she'd have killed me on sight. And judging from her threat, which I very much believed, she hadn't yet ruled out that possibility. So why drag it out? Why reveal that she spoke my language? Why do whatever it was she was planning to do?

Through the gaps in the wooden stakes, I caught a glimpse of her lithe form, illuminated by the faint glow of luminescent plants scattered throughout the village. She moved with purpose, with both her steps and actions chosen carefully, presumably so she didn't wake anyone else. It was a while before I realized I'd been staring openmouthed, and I quickly shut it, disgusted with myself.

You hate her. Look what she put you through. She's keeping you from Cedric.

But the longer I kept watching her, my gaze trailing her every move, the farther my brother and his plight drifted from my mind.

It was a few minutes before she returned, emerging from the darkness in that silent way of hers. If the shadows hadn't reacted to her presence, I may have once again wondered if she were even real. I didn't believe in things such as spirits or ghosts, but the faint glow of her paint made her look so otherworldly that it may have been enough to convince me on the spot. Oblivious to all that was running through my mind, she set to work quickly, kneeling before the cage before glancing around to make certain we were alone.

Only then did I bother to glance at what she clutched in her arms: rags that appeared to have been soaked in water, a separate wrapped bundle whose contents I couldn't make out, and a small bucket. She set down everything but the rags before beckoning me closer with a crook of her finger, but I refused to move other than to raise an eyebrow.

"No more silence or gestures. If you can talk, *talk*."

She returned my glare. "I hate English."

"¿Hablas español?" I asked, but given the confusion on her face, the answer to that was no. "I wish I spoke your language, but given that I don't, it seems English is our only option."

"Or you could just do what I say and don't ask questions."

"You'd like that, wouldn't you?" I shot back before I could help myself. "If you think that's the type of person I am, you don't know me very well."

"On the contrary, Elvira Teach"—the way she said my name

turned my blood to ice—"I know exactly who you are. And so does everyone else in this village."

My mind raced as it worked to catch up, because while this was a possibility I'd never considered, it made perfect, sickening sense. Of *course* she knew who I was, because the natives must have been watching us for much longer than we'd realized. And if she knew who I was, that meant…

"You know my brother," I forced out, more a statement than a question, but she nodded all the same as her lips twisted into a snarl.

"Cedric Teach," she spat, and I lunged forward, slamming against and gripping the stakes so hard my knuckles turned white. She didn't flinch.

"If you think for one second that I'd *ever* betray him, you're better off just killing me now." I locked my gaze with hers, desperately trying to ignore her breaths caressing my skin. "Our bond goes far deeper than the blood we share."

She regarded me coolly, setting her jaw into a hard line. "We know, Serpent."

That caught me off guard. "Then… what do you want with me?"

Silence stretched between us, but she finally replied, "To keep you away from him."

Understanding dawned on me then. "So he…" my voice trailed off, and I couldn't complete my sentence.

So he dies.

She fell silent once again, though why she was unwilling to at least confirm it, I didn't know. I didn't move away from the stakes, but I hung my head slightly, causing my hair to fall over my face. Good. I didn't need her to see my weakness, couldn't allow her to know how much I truly cared for my brother, that I couldn't envision what my world might look like without Cedric in it. I still didn't know why she'd kept me alive—that was the only way to know for certain I'd never return to him—but I no longer cared. I had the answers I needed, and it was more than enough fuel to keep loathing her with every ounce of strength I still possessed.

My body apparently had other ideas, because I was caught off guard a second time when she reached out to cover my hands with hers. An involuntary shudder ran through me, and despite wanting to with every fiber of my being, I didn't pull away. "Look at me," she commanded, and I did.

"I have rags for you to clean yourself. Food"—she nodded toward the bundle—"and water. But don't overindulge, because the others can't know I helped you. It will be easy enough to lie and say the rat wandered in here on its own, but beyond that, you can't look too healthy. Understood?"

"Why?" The word tumbled out before I could stop it. "Why are you doing this?"

Her face hardened, and she withdrew her hands. "Do you want my help?"

No. The part of me that still wanted to kill her nearly blurted it out, but I bit my tongue just in time, nodding weakly instead.

"Then eat, Elvira."

She passed me the bundle, but I pushed it away, shaking my

head and pointing toward the bucket instead. "Water first."

It was difficult to grip it properly given how my hands were bound, but the moment I managed to balance the bucket's weight, I began guzzling down the water as fast as I could without choking. The cool liquid felt like a medicine in itself, soothing my parched throat as it went down while providing much-needed clarity to my still sluggish mind. With each swallow, I felt far more like myself, and by the time I finished, I'd drained more than half the bucket's contents.

I wasn't surprised that she sat there and watched me in what was now a familiar routine between us. Though that guarded expression was back when she took the bucket from me, I didn't miss that glimmer of interest she tried so hard to hide as she offered the bundle once again. "Eat."

Now that my thirst had been quenched, the ravenous hunger gnawing at my belly immediately sprang to the surface. I tore into the wrappings and shoved its contents into my mouth without even bothering to look at what I was eating. An unfamiliar flavor flooded my mouth, but not a bad one, and the texture told me it was some sort of meat. Though it was a bit dry, I was far too hungry to care, and once it was gone, I was almost tempted to ask for more.

Before I could utter a word, though, she shoved the wet rags into my hands. "To get clean," she explained when I cocked a brow in confusion. "But not too much, or they'll notice. Just to be more…"

"Comfortable?" I guessed when her voice trailed off.

It was difficult to tell in such dim light, but I could have sworn a blush crept to her cheeks. "Yes. Comfortable."

She kept staring as I got to work, her gaze intense and unwavering, as if trying to discern something in my expression or read my thoughts. I ignored her, too focused on cleaning off the dirt and grime that had been caked onto my skin for days now. Though I couldn't wash it all away, even being able to do what little she allowed brought a fresh wave of relief, and my body relaxed beneath my own touch.

There was a rather stubborn spot on my face, though, near my forehead, and it was bothering me given that there was hair stuck to it. I scrubbed and scrubbed, but to no avail. Not only was the angle awkward, lacking full range of motion in my hands on top of it made what I was trying to do nearly impossible.

I froze when once again, her fingers curled around mine. "Let me," she whispered, almost imperceptibly soft, and I didn't protest or fight when she took the rag. It was as if she had me in a trance, and I remained still as she resumed. Unlike the way I'd furiously, borderline violently rubbed at the spot, her approach was the opposite. She simply held the cloth there and still while we sat seemingly suspended in time. Her dark eyes were locked onto mine, as unreadable as ever, yet something within them made my heart flutter faster. The warmth from her fingers spread across my cheek, and before I knew what I was doing or why, I leaned into her touch.

Conflicting urges began warring within me, and there was no way to tell which was stronger. On one hand, she was the reason I was a captive and being kept away from Cedric. She could be the reason he *died*. She'd drugged me, bound me, and let me suffer in agonizing, indescribable pain for nearly two days before doing anything about it. I wanted to kill her for what she'd done. I hated her.

But another part of me—a part that only grew stronger with each passing second—desperately wanted to kiss her.

Time slowed nearly to a halt, especially when she brought her free hand to my chin, grasping it with more force than I expected. My mouth parted in shock, and the next thing I knew…

Nothing. I knew nothing, because surely we'd slipped into a dream. There was no other explanation for how her lips had found their way to mine, or mine to hers—I couldn't be certain. But dream or not, she wasn't simply kissing me back. She was drinking me in, devouring me in ways no one ever had before, and more surprisingly, I was letting her. I surrendered both to her touch and tongue, moaning into her mouth as she explored every inch of mine.

Almost as quickly as it began, the kiss was suddenly over. She pulled away and scrambled upright clumsily, nearly losing her balance as she frantically worked to gather up any and all evidence that she'd ever been here. I blinked in bewilderment, but there was no denying what we'd just done. Not when the taste of her still lingered on my lips.

"W-wait," I stammered, only remembering to keep my voice down at the last moment. "I don't even know your name."

She hesitated for the briefest of moments, but refused to meet my gaze as something heavy and unspoken hovered in the air between us. Stepping back, her lithe form was silhouetted against the faint glow of the moonlight filtering through the trees above. The swallow's feather in her hair shimmered with an ethereal light, casting a halo around her face as she lingered, and for a moment, it seemed possible she might stay.

But without a sound, she turned and slipped into the darkness, leaving me alone once more with my tumultuous thoughts. The memory of her touch still burned upon my skin, as did the feel of her against my lips. As I watched her go, an uncomfortable weight settled deep in my chest—pain that had nothing to do with the rot that still lingered within me, and everything to do with the woman who had saved my life.

Who had *kissed* me.

I sat back, forcing myself to swallow the lump in my throat. Now that she was gone, the sounds of the forest echoed around me on all sides, including several Nightstalker screams. Cold stabbed at my skin, only intensified by the wet rags I'd run over myself mere moments before, and I shuddered in the blackness. But before the chill could fully consume me, a voice no louder than a whisper sliced through, cleaner than any knife.

"My name is Blue Feather."

V. THE FIGHT

I couldn't sleep, even as the hours trickled by. The only reason I'd been able to previously was because of how weak I'd been and how exhausted fighting the curse had left me, but now that I was healed, my thoughts were as loud as they were relentless. They drifted back to Cedric and even Scarlett, to the events of the past several days, and of course to my plight and how I might get out of it.

Mostly, though, they were fixated on *her*.

I still wasn't entirely used to her name, elegant as it was: Blue Feather. It had to be a translation from her native tongue to English, or perhaps she didn't yet trust me with her true name, and had given a false one. It didn't bother me, though. It was something to call her, something to caress with my tongue as I wished I'd done with her lips, something to—

"No," I hissed aloud, forcing my eyes open in an effort to snap myself out of the irritatingly alluring mental image my mind had conjured. "You want to kill her, remember? And you *will* kill her as soon as you get out of this."

There was quite a lot I wanted to do to her, apparently, but I forced myself to focus on the more violent bits. Choking the life out of her, holding a knife to that slender throat, forcing her to her knees before slicing said throat… but that would be a waste, wouldn't it? I could think of far better uses for a girl on her knees.

What the fuck is wrong with you, Elvira?

If I was being honest, it was little wonder the lines were becoming so blurred with her. Fighting and fucking had never felt much different, and it wasn't like I hadn't mixed pleasure and duty before. But this *was* different—Cedric's life was on the line, and he didn't have time for me to give in to such hedonistic desires, no matter how much I wanted to. Clenching my teeth, I dug my fingernails into my palms in an attempt to clear my thoughts. Blue Feather may have healed me, but I didn't believe for one second I was any safer now than I was prior to the rat. I had to keep my wits about me. I had to focus.

I had to fight.

Fueled by a surge of determination, I sat up and glanced around. I needed out of this damn cage, but first, I had to free my hands.

Though they still held firm, the rope bindings around my wrists had become saturated with whatever liquid had started leaking from my pores during the worst of the rot. Disgusting, yes, but hopefully it had weakened the fibers, and if I could loosen them enough, perhaps I could free myself. It was the best and only hope I had, considering there wasn't anything sharp anywhere within my reach. Taking a deep breath, I rubbed my hands together as hard as I could in an effort to create some friction. My own labored breathing as well as more Nightstalker screams pounded relentlessly in my ears as I worked, and angry red welts began appearing on the outer edges of my poor wrists, but eventually, the rope started to give way.

My grin of triumph quickly vanished as my senses screamed a warning. I snapped my head up once again, not at noise, but at… silence. Eerie, sudden silence, the type you couldn't trust in Neverland. The shrieks had gone quiet all at once, leaving in their place an oppressive stillness that hung in the air like a thick fog. Shivers shot down my spine as my body reacted to what my mind already knew, but was unwilling to believe until I glimpsed it with my own eyes.

When I swiveled my head, there they were: Nightstalkers, dozens of them, creeping through the shadows like the pack of hungry wolves they'd once been prior to their monstrous transformation, their yellow eyes shining with an unnerving glow. They surrounded the camp on all sides in what appeared to be an organized formation, and were rapidly closing in.

My heart began beating against my ribcage as panic took hold.

It was just before dawn, but as far as I could tell, the camp remained asleep and completely unaware of the danger they were in. Where were the guards? Surely these people had traps or other defenses—they wouldn't have survived this long otherwise—so why weren't any of them activating? Was I truly the only one seeing this, the only one who could warn them?

It wasn't a question of whether I should, because my personal feelings aside, no one deserved to get ripped apart by Nightstalkers. It was a question of *how*, because not only was I still trapped in this cage, I was completely defenseless. I couldn't run, couldn't hide, and I could barely move given that my hands remained bound. I could scream, but not only was that likely to get me killed, I didn't know how many, if any, of the natives would hear me at this distance.

My time to think came to a shattering halt when one of the beasts set its sights on me. Breaking away from the main group, a Nightstalker made its way toward me, baring its fangs even as maggots writhed between its teeth. Instinct had me scrambling to the back of my cage, and my mind was made up in an instant.

I shrieked at the top of my lungs.

Almost immediately, human shouts answered my call, but there wasn't time to be relieved that someone had heard me—not when a second Nightstalker came barreling in my direction as fast as its rotting legs could carry it. Resigning to my helplessness, I squeezed my eyes shut and braced for the inevitable impact of antlers impaling the cage, me, or both… but it never came. When animalistic snarls broke out from somewhere in front of me, I dared a peek, and it took a moment to piece together the writhing bodies rolling around in the mud. It seemed the two Nightstalkers who had spotted me were now fighting over who got to claim me as their prize, but at least for now, I was safe.

Sitting up a little straighter, I turned my sights to the village, stifling yet another cry. The first wave of Nightstalkers had already invaded the camp, and it was chaos. Though several warriors were bravely and successfully facing off with a few of the beasts, there weren't nearly enough of them to make up for the sheer number of monsters now ravaging their home. The Nightstalkers tore through the village with more violence than a pack of hogs, ripping open huts and overturning baskets of food and supplies. It soon became obvious why there were so few people present; the warriors were the only ones who remained. Though unclear where the rest of the villagers had gone, I hoped more than anything they were safe—but there was one warrior I had yet to glimpse.

I scanned the village twice over, but there was no sign of Blue Feather. Perhaps she was guarding the children and elders, but my gut knew better; there was no way she wouldn't be out here, slaughtering Nightstalkers and actively defending her home. Then where in Adais's name was she?

Unable to hold it in any longer, I screamed her name just as the first rays of sunrise began peeking through the gaps in the trees. I'd attract the attention of more Nightstalkers, no doubt, but I didn't care. I wanted to know she was alive.

I *needed* to know she was alive.

No sooner had I opened my mouth to cry out again, something dark and furry slammed against my cage with so much force it was a wonder that, save for several audible *cracks*, the stakes held firm. I shied back, eyes wide with panic as the dazed Nighstalker came to its senses. My mind scrambled to form a plan in the precious few seconds I possessed, but came up with nothing; I had nowhere to go and no way to defend myself. As if it could sense my fear, the Nighstalker sprang up a moment later and lunged at the cage, antlers first, and I shrieked as the impact rattled my bones.

The beast struck again and again, with each hit causing the wood to creak and groan under its weight until finally, one of the stakes gave out with an ear-splitting *snap*. I only barely managed to dart out away as the stake fell forward, trapping me in an even smaller space, and now the beast had direct access to gore me, rip me to shreds, or both.

I turned away, flinching at the Nightstalker's snarl. But before I'd so much as closed my eyes, a cry sounded from close by: a human cry.

Her cry.

The noise soon mingled with the Nightstalker's as it bellowed a deafening roar, and when it whirled around, there was an arrow buried deep in its flank. Two more found their mark before Blue Feather reached us, but the beast wasn't slowed; if anything, she had only enraged it. Tossing her bow aside, she drew a dagger in each hand as the Nightstalker charged, but she was more than ready. Ducking beneath its antlers in what was clearly a practiced maneuver, she sliced both blades along its underside as it continued to charge forward, and didn't stop even as blood splattered across her face. The beast roared in agony as she slipped from beneath it, and a moment later, its insides came tumbling out, spilling into the mud as it collapsed in a twitching heap.

It was only when Blue Feather turned to me that I realized I'd been staring openmouthed, but I didn't bother to shut it. I couldn't. I'd never doubted her capabilities as a warrior, but seeing her in action was another thing entirely—seeing her covered in *blood* was another thing entirely. The crimson intermingled with her war paint, the colors contrasting yet complementing one another at the same time. She'd tied her hair back for battle, but that swallow's feather remained, dangling in front of her right ear like always.

"Elvira," she barked sharply, and I could tell by her tone it wasn't the first time she'd said my name. Blinking, I met her gaze, prompting her to continue. "Are you all right?"

I nodded, and she grunted in response before sheathing one of the daggers back at her thigh. Once she'd retrieved her bow, Blue Feather set her sights on what was left of my cage, carefully removing the broken stake before reaching inside and extending a hand to me. "Be careful. These edges are sharp."

Touching any part of her seemed like a mistake, but it wasn't as if I had any other choice. I gripped her hand with both of mine, trying desperately to ignore the tingles erupting from where our skin made contact as she pulled me from the cage. A sigh escaped my lips when I stepped outside, at last free of my prison of more than two days, but I couldn't have celebrated even if I wanted to. The village remained under attack, and though it was difficult to tell, it appeared the natives might be losing.

What's more, there remained the question of what Blue Feather intended to do with me. Was she about to drag me off to yet another prison? Tie me up somewhere else? Finally kill me, just as she'd threatened on more than one occasion?

I tensed when she yanked me close—so close that we were pressed up against one another—but before I could protest, in one fluid motion, she sliced away my bindings. As the ropes fell away and into the dirt, I made a noise that was somewhere between surprise and relief as I rubbed my aching wrists, careful to avoid the welts.

Something flashed across Blue Feather's face, but it was gone a moment later. We remained in closer proximity than we'd ever been, our forms pressed tightly to one another as an increasingly bloody fight raged around us, and though I wanted badly to speak, the countless questions I wanted to voice turned to ash in my mouth.

Why did you free me? Does that mean I can return to Cedric? What will happen to you if I go—will you be all right? Why do I care?

Do you know *that I care?*

Blue Feather spoke first, her tone hoarse and strained. "Elvira, I—"

"Look out!"

I shoved against her chest with enough force to knock her to the ground, but it had the desired effect. The Nightstalker I'd only noticed in the last handful of seconds raked its claws across empty air rather than where Blue Feather had just stood. It was a moment before the beast pieced together that it had missed, but

Blue Feather recovered faster. Yelling my name once more, she tossed me her dagger the moment she had my attention—thank Adais I caught it by the handle—before whipping out the second she'd previously sheathed at her thigh.

Without another word, we charged the beast, with Blue Feather closing in on the left while I went right. Our fighting styles were very different, but complemented one another well enough that the Nightstalker couldn't decide which one of us was the bigger threat. While Blue Feather kept her body low to the ground, seemingly prepared to repeat her earlier trick, I remained upright, looking the ugly thing right in its beady little eye as I lunged. The creature snarled, snapping at both of us, but that was its mistake. Blue Feather drew first blood, managing to inflict a nasty slice across its flank, but I was the one to finish it. With a roar of my own, I plunged my dagger into the beast's neck, twisting for good measure even as it made a weak attempt to bite my upper arm. As I yanked the blade from its flesh, Blue Feather came to stand beside me, panting as hard as I was. We watched the Nightstalker slump to the ground, and didn't look away until it stopped twitching for good.

Blue Feather was about to speak, but got cut off once again when a yell sounded from behind us. She sprinted off without hesitation, and though it briefly crossed my mind to run in the opposite direction and escape this place for good, I couldn't just leave her— not like this. So with gritted teeth, I followed close on Blue Feather's heels, prepared for more Nightstalkers to leap out at any moment.

She led us deep into the village, navigating through the maze of Nightstalker corpses that littered the ground with unnerving precision. Many of the beasts had fallen, but many still remained, and the warriors left standing seemed barely able to do so. Blood seeped into the dirt, forming dozens of tiny crimson rivers that crisscrossed and even formed entire puddles. More than once, I stepped in one, and hissed in irritation as it splattered up my front. I'd *just* cleaned myself.

After dodging several more warriors and the Nightstalkers they battled, we at last reached our destination: the male warrior who'd taunted me on my very first day here had one of his legs trapped beneath a dead Nightstalker. His already wide gaze widened even more upon glimpsing me, but he quickly fixated on Blue Feather, and they exchanged a few words in their language. He wanted us to help him, but how we'd manage that, I had no idea. Even the smallest Nightstalkers weighed the same as half a dozen men.

This one wasn't small.

"We can't," I hissed to Blue Feather, for once hoping her friend didn't speak English. "And even if we could, there's no way that leg is salvageable."

She whirled around and spoke with so much venom that I took a step back. "Who said anything about 'we?' None of this is your fight, or your problem. Get the fuck out of here while you still have a chance. GO!"

Blue Feather's words did the opposite, with shock rooting me in place as I watched her try in vain to free the trapped warrior. Was that what she truly wanted—for me to leave? And why was she angry that I hadn't? She'd been perfectly happy to fight by my side mere minutes ago, and had seen the truth as clearly as I had. No matter how much we didn't want to admit it, for right now, we were far better off remaining together. If I ran off, I had about as good a chance of making my escape as I did being eaten alive by a Nightstalker.

Maybe that's it. She's too much of a coward to kill you herself, so she's hoping the forest will do it for her.

That made up my mind, and after snarling something along the lines of "I'm not fucking leaving," I knelt at Blue Feather's side. We worked together, our combined strength and determination managing to shift the dead Nightstalker little by little. It was no easy task. The beast was far larger than the ones we had killed earlier, and we were in far more danger here than we'd been in the outskirts of the village. The battle raged around us, the warrior's breath came in shorter and shorter gasps, and I was nearly convinced we'd never manage to free him, but at last, we shifted the corpse enough to where he was able to wiggle free.

The leg was mangled, likely beyond repair. But I didn't say a word as I helped Blue Feather drag him to the safety of a nearby hut, and he even flashed me a weak smile before we retreated, grunting a few words.

"He says thank you," Blue Feather translated quietly. Judging from her tone, I suspected he wasn't the only one who was grateful, but I didn't voice the thought aloud. We lingered in the doorway, and though Blue Feather didn't say anything else, the question in her eyes was loud and clear: *Will you stay, or will you go?*

I didn't answer with words, and charged back into the fray with a fierce battle cry. Blue Feather followed close behind, and together, we helped drive off the remaining Nightstalkers. The village may be in shambles, but victory was imminent if only we could hold them off for just a little longer. Time seemed to blur as we fought, our bodies drenched in sweat and blood—some of it our own, but mostly that of the Nightstalkers. I hacked and slashed, channeling all my rage and frustration into my blade as it sliced through sinew and bone alike. Blue Feather was never far from my side, and we settled into a frenzied rhythm, watching one another's backs as we worked as a team.

As… partners.

The realization only fueled my anger, and I fought harder, determined to shove away the conflicting emotions that threatened to overwhelm me. My body ached from exhaustion, yet I refused to stop or slow, both to keep from facing what I didn't want to acknowledge and because I didn't want Blue Feather to think me weak. Before long, we had the beasts on the run, and she remained close as we tailed their fleeing shapes well past the village's borders. The chase was exhilarating, but when we finally lost sight of them, my dread returned the instant we slowed to a halt.

Not only were we alone once more, our current setting was more beautiful than it had any right to be. We stood in a small, intimate clearing, surrounded on all sides by vegetation so thick it would be nearly impossible for anything, even a Nightstalker, to slip through unnoticed. A few paces ahead, a stream babbled, but that wasn't where my gaze was drawn. The clearing's main feature were the hundreds of blue flowers growing anywhere and everywhere, with each plant emitting a faint but steady luminescent glow.

Blue Feather whispered something I didn't catch, but repeated herself when I turned to face her. "Nizhano," she said, gesturing to the flowers. "It's what we call them. They're sacred."

"And you use them to make your paint?" The question slipped out before I could stop it, but she only nodded before doubling over to catch her breath.

As tempted as I was to do the same given the burning in my own chest, I didn't want to take my eyes off her even for a second. We may have just fought as allies, but not only had Blue Feather proven herself a force to be reckoned with, she still looked every bit the lethal predator my instincts screamed at me to fear. So much blood coated her face and body that her war paint was barely visible—even her feather hadn't been spared—and her clothes were torn and ruined. She'd kept a tight hold on her dagger, and though her bow remained slung over her back, no doubt she'd be ready to fire it at a moment's notice.

A heavy silence enveloped us when Blue Feather looked up, seemingly as she, too, remembered what we were to each other. Her gaze flicked to my bloodied dagger and back again, asking yet another question without words: *Now that the battle is over, what do you intend to do with that?*

Before I could conjure an answer, she took a few steps forward, slowly closing the distance between us. Chills shot down my spine, but I could no longer tell if they were from exhilaration or fear; it all felt the same with her. Did she scare me so much that I somehow found it attractive? Or was she so attractive that it was scaring me?

Was there even a difference?

Blue Feather halted within arm's reach, but didn't move or say anything. Even if she had, I wouldn't have heard it over the blood roaring in my ears. Another rush of adrenaline coursed through me as our eyes met, and it became impossible to hide my quivering, undoubtedly from anticipation. Was she about to kiss or stab me? It could be either, especially given that she hadn't dropped her knife.

I flinched when she raised a hand—but not the one with the blade. She froze for the briefest of moments, but cupped my face when I didn't move away or protest, tracing her thumb across my bottom lip. "Are you all right?"

Finding words was difficult with her this close—with her *touching* me—but somehow I managed it. "Y-yes. Fine."

Blue Feather tightened her grip, keeping me rooted in place in more ways than one. "You're certain?"

I nodded this time, not trusting myself to speak, but she didn't like that. Digging her fingernails into my skin, she yanked me close, ignoring my yelp of surprise. "Use your words, Elvira."

That awakened something within me, but perhaps not what she'd intended to provoke. Swallowing back my snarl, I instead tightened my grip on my dagger, barely managing to keep my voice even as I spoke. "Careful. I'm not the obedient type."

"Was that a threat?" Blue Feather's voice went deadly quiet, and while I didn't look down, there was suddenly something sharp against my throat.

"No," I said simply. "But this is."

Then I lunged.

VI. THE CLEARING

I expected far more resistance when I slammed into Blue Feather's front. Instead, gravity caught us both off guard, and we went careening to the ground in a tangled heap of limbs and blades. Blue Feather took the worst of it, landing on her back with the wind knocked from her. I recovered faster, but only just. She rolled to the side at precisely the right time, and my dagger plunged into dirt rather than where her heart had been a moment before.

"Fuck," I hissed, but then cried out as Blue Feather's knee plunged into my groin hard enough to cause my vision to go dark for a split second. She slipped from under me, and I only had enough time to yank my blade free before leaping upright to face her once more.

Her breath came in strained huffs as she eyed me, and all that cool indifference vanished. It wasn't shock or even anger written all over her face; Blue Feather looked downright murderous, and when she spoke, there was an edge to her voice that I hadn't heard before. "You've been waiting a long time to do that."

It wasn't a question, but I nodded anyway. "Been fantasizing about it for days, little swallow."

"I'm far from little," Blue Feather snapped.

"You're littler than me." As we spoke, we circled one another, weapons held down at our sides—for now.

She narrowed her gaze, clearly thinking hard about her reply. "And you're good at getting a rise out of people, which is why you tacked on that last bit… but the first is far more interesting. What else have you been fantasizing about, *Serpent*?"

The emphasis on my nickname sent chills up my spine, but I lifted my chin and spoke through gritted teeth. "The way you'll beg for your pathetic life before I end it."

I wasn't prepared for the sudden shift in Blue Feather's tone and demeanor. She raised an eyebrow, and her voice was low… borderline sultry. "If I ever beg you for anything, I assure you, it won't be for my life."

Oh, fuck.

The mental image her words conjured was almost too much to bear, and it wasn't easy to suppress my traitorous body's shudder. Even now, she saw right through me and my façade, through the conflicting emotions I had yet to gain full control over. I wanted to kill her—that much was clear.

But perhaps even more, I simply wanted *her*.

Having kept a close eye on my every move, Blue Feather didn't miss when my gaze shot to her lips. It was the briefest of glances, and I caught myself right away, but she smirked regardless. "Fantasizing about the kiss, too? If you'd like another, all you have to do is ask."

With another snarl, I lunged again, but this time, she was ready.

A flash of silver was my only warning. Blue Feather stood her ground but twisted her body to the side. Her blade came up in one swift motion, and when I slipped past her, she managed to slash me across my upper arm, ripping through the fabric of my shirt and drawing blood. I cried out but immediately bit my tongue; it stung, but I'd had far worse.

When I whirled back around, Blue Feather was back in a defensive stance but didn't look nearly as smug as I expected. It pissed me off even more. "Oh, *now* you're tired of taunting me?"

"Of course I'm tired, and I know you are, too." She shook her head, sighing until her shoulders sagged. "I'm hungry, I'm exhausted, and I don't want to fight, especially not with you. I don't want to hurt you. I want…"

Only when her voice trailed off did I realize I'd been hanging on to every word. "What do you want?"

Blue Feather shot me a glare. "Forget me. What do *you* want? If it's to go back to your murderer of a brother, then what are you waiting for? Go, just like I told you in the village."

"As if you wouldn't shoot me the moment I turned my back."

"Do you truly believe that I would—"

"You've been threatening as much for days!"

"—or is that just the excuse you're telling yourself?" Blue Feather finished, completely ignoring my outburst. "And don't insult me. I don't shoot prey when its back is turned, not even Nightstalkers."

I stiffened. "Is that what I am to you? Prey?"

"You're avoiding the question," she pressed. "Both questions, actually. But since I already know the answers, I'll spare you the torture of having to say it and ask another. Why do you want to die so badly, Elvira Teach?"

The ache in my arm was suddenly nothing compared to the pain her words summoned, and it swirled in my gut, clawing at my insides just as the rot had done all this time. I squeezed my eyes shut, and my reply was hoarse. "I don—"

"Yes, you do. I knew it from the moment I saw you come out of that forest, desperate, weak, and alone. You claimed you had your reasons, but if this was truly about saving Cedric, you'd have gone back to him by now. You haven't, which means—"

"Don't," I hissed, rage boiling beneath my skin once more. "Another word about Cedric and I'll slice out your tongue."

Blue Feather opened her mouth then shut it again. A hush descended over the clearing as we glowered at one another, and even the nearby stream lowered its noise to a whisper, as if it, too, wanted to know how this would end. All the while, my mind raced, more conflicted than ever. On one hand, I had half a mind to hurl my dagger at her infuriating face. On the other… she was right.

The only reason I was still here was because deep down, I didn't think Cedric was going to make it. If he wasn't dead already, he would be soon; not only was that something I couldn't bear to watch, I was even more afraid of what came after.

Of being alone.

Cedric had Scarlett, but I had no one. Not since Jasper, and whatever we'd shared was nothing to boast about. He'd been claimed by the forest shortly after our arrival in Neverland. I missed him, yes, but mostly, I missed fucking him. I thought Jasper had known me better than anyone else in this world, anyone apart from Cedric, but in all the years we'd spent together, he'd never understood me half as well as Blue Feather had in only a matter of days.

And I *hated* her for it. How had all that silence, innumerable glares and glances, and a handful of empty threats become this— whatever there was between us? How had it led us to kiss, to touch, to fight at one another's side as if we'd trained together all our lives?

How was it that I only wanted more?

"Elvira?" It was Blue Feather's tone rather than the sound of her voice that pulled me from my thoughts. "Are you all—"

"Don't you dare ask if I'm all right. This is your fault."

She visibly stiffened. "Interrupt me one more time, and I swear—"

"You'll what, cut me again?" I spread my arms in a mock challenge, causing blood to seep down my elbow. "Go right ahead."

I hadn't even finished my sentence before Blue Feather was on me, and this time, I barely put up a fight. Exhaustion had caught up to my body and mind alike, and once she'd wrestled the dagger from my grip, she had me pinned in a matter of seconds. Other than her blade at my throat, it was more comfortable than I wanted to admit. The grass was soft against my back and wounded arm, and her weight on top of me, her groin pressed against mine…

This woman was going to be the death of me, and from the look in her eyes, she knew it. A smirk played on her lips once she had my wrists pinned above my head with her free hand, and she used the other to trace the tip of her dagger across my irritatingly sensitive skin. I bit my lip to keep from gasping, but there was no reining in my body's reaction. My back arched, seeking friction in all the right places, and soon, she had me writhing beneath her.

Blue Feather kept up what she was doing, though she did grow increasingly amused. "See? All you had to do was tell me what you want."

She didn't cease exploring my body with the knife, but she did up the pressure. I flinched at first, fully convinced she'd sliced me open a second time, but a glance at my collarbone, where the blade now hovered just beneath the neckline of my shirt, informed me she hadn't.

I looked up then and was wholly unprepared for what I saw in Blue Feather's gaze. "Use your words, Elvira." That same command— this time in an entirely different context. "Tell me what you want."

I wanted so much that I wasn't sure where to begin. Add that to the fact my breaths were coming in shorter gasps, and all I managed between breathless pants was, "You. I want *you*."

Blue Feather didn't need to be told twice. The pressure on my wrists vanished a moment later, but before I could do anything with my newfound freedom, a hand snaked beneath my shirt, cupping one of my breasts in a brutal squeeze. I cried out, but more in surprise than pain, especially when the ache only added to my building arousal. She reached to give my other breast the same treatment before pinching my nipple, and at that, I hissed.

She frowned. "Too much?"

"Not enough," I growled, and reached to shove her off me. Shock crossed Blue Feather's face a moment before I straddled her instead, and my hips ground against hers in a steady but urgent rhythm as I fumbled with my shirt. I winced when it came time to free my bloodied arm from its sleeve, but then it was off, and the sting became little more than a dull throb as I guided Blue Feather's hands back to my breasts. "Squeeze me. *Hard.*"

Her lust-filled gaze met mine as she obliged, and I threw my head to the sky, relishing the cool night air at my back and Blue Feather's warmth at my front. My hands moved of their own accord, roaming over her body as I tugged at the strings of her leather vest. The fabric loosened, and I used it to pull her closer as I leaned in to brush my lips against hers. She tasted like blood and victory, and I wanted more. My tongue sought out hers as my hands continued their exploration beneath the vest I couldn't wait to get off.

I felt Blue Feather's moan before I heard it, and that only spurred me on further. My fingers grazed the waist of her pants before hooking inside, but before I could go any farther, she wrapped an arm around my middle to anchor me in place. "Not yet," she breathed against my neck as she pulled away just enough to look me in the eye. "You first."

Agonizingly slowly, she trailed her fingers down the space between my breasts, my stomach, and then they were *there*, slipping inside my pants and settling at the core of my arousal. I closed my eyes as a moan slipped from my lips but opened them when Blue Feather clicked her tongue. "You'll ride me with your eyes open."

So I did. She was patient, even though she obviously didn't need to be, and waited until her fingers were well coated with my slickness before slipping one inside. That lasted only a few seconds before a second joined it, and I inhaled sharply, my hips moving involuntarily as my inner walls clenched around her. Blue Feather's mouth curved into a satisfied grin, and she moved in a slow but steady rhythm that had me gasping her name within moments.

My hands flew to her shoulders when her thumb found my clit, and I clung to her for dear life as our breathing turned ragged. The forced eye contact was as delicious as it was infuriating. I longed to bury my face in her neck, to conceal what she was doing to me, but it was far too late for that. Her movements grew more insistent with each passing second until I could stand it no longer, and with another cry, she sent me over the edge. My body trembled against hers as the orgasm ripped through me, and only when I ceased trembling did Blue Feather withdraw.

Despite myself, I whimpered, but I silenced when the tip of her knife was against my throat once more. She dragged it from my neck to my collarbone, and finally to my breasts, tracing a lazy circle around my nipple while her free hand knotted in my hair, yanking my head back to expose even more of me. It was everything I could do to keep still, especially given that every nerve ending in my body was on fire.

"Serpents have a rather interesting tongue," Blue Feather whispered in my ear, and I bit my lip to keep from moaning again. "Do you know how to use yours?"

Her words ignited something within me—something primal. With strength I didn't know I still possessed, I wrestled the dagger from her grip before shoving her to the ground, yanking her clothes off in a frenzy. Blue Feather's eyes widened, but she didn't fight when I tore away the leather vest and pants that had kept her so tantalizingly out of reach. My hands roamed over her body as she lay helpless beneath me, and I explored her just as I had in my dreams these past few nights.

It wasn't for her pleasure, though: it was for mine, and mine alone. Though I didn't use it as she had, I kept the dagger close, ready to snatch it at a moment's notice. I was rough with her, rougher even than she had been with me, and every sound that escaped her lips, whether it was a groan of pleasure or cry of pain, flooded me with satisfaction. I squeezed, slapped, and clawed at every inch of skin I could reach, but I didn't do the one thing she'd asked for, and the increasingly frustrated looks she shot me told me it was working.

"Are you punishing me," Blue Feather managed between breathless pants, "or yourself?"

Both. Her for bringing me to orgasm, and me for letting her. Her for being so good with her hands, with her mouth, and me for enjoying it. Her for tearing down my walls, leaving me broken and exposed, and me for putting them up in the first place.

Her for looking so damn good with her face flushed, her hair tangled and in disarray, and the loathing in her eyes.

And me for wanting to fuck her into oblivion.

With a frustrated snarl, I snatched the dagger, letting it hover over her heart once more. Blue Feather held my gaze but made no move to stop me. "Still have no idea what you want, I see," she said coolly.

"I want to hear you scream," I snapped. "I'm just not sure what *kind* of scream, and that's been the problem all along."

She shrugged, keeping up that calm demeanor. "You could always fuck me and then kill me. But if you kill me first… well, that's the end."

"Or," I said, mimicking her irritating impassiveness as I trailed the dagger down her chest and stomach, finally coming to a halt just below her hips, "I could fuck you *with* this and accomplish both at the same time."

Blue Feather's eyes widened at that, and she squirmed beneath me. "You wouldn't—"

She silenced abruptly when I brought the blade between her thighs, and flinched when it touched her. But it wasn't the end she'd been expecting, and she relaxed almost immediately. I moved the handle in slow circles, teasing at her entrance, and feeling how wet she was only summoned more of my own arousal. Watching her face carefully, I waited until she wasn't looking before flipping the blade and continuing my exploration with the sharp end. Blue Feather jumped again, but I held her firm and steady, shaking my head as slowly as I moved the knife. Once its edge was thoroughly coated in her wetness, I brought it to my lips, running my tongue across it as I held her lust-filled gaze. Her taste was strong and earthy, and it sent another jolt of arousal straight to my groin.

"I may be cruel," I told her honestly, lowering the blade back down. "But I return my favors."

I didn't wait for her to respond before sliding the handle inside her, savoring her tightness, but was always mindful of the sharp end in my hand. Keeping her legs apart with both of mine, I moved the handle back and forth, pushing deeper with each thrust until it was almost entirely inside her. Blue Feather bit down on her bottom lip as she watched me, but every now and then a tiny whimper would slip out. Not a scream, but there was still plenty of time for that.

Increasing the pace gradually, I matched the speed of my thrusts to the moans she could no longer stifle as I built up to an urgent rhythm. Leaning down, I kissed and licked her nipples, teasing them with my tongue as I drove the dagger ever deeper. This alone nearly sent her over the edge; Blue Feather's hips rocked in time with mine as she tangled her fingers in my hair, guiding my mouth to where she wanted it. Her body grew slick with saliva and sweat alike, and her cries grew louder as I thrust faster and harder.

By the time I withdrew the dagger and replaced it with my

fingers, she needed only the smallest nudge before she came apart. Her back arched, requesting the friction I was eager to give her, and Blue Feather's scream was swallowed by the forest as her climax hit her hard and fast. I claimed her lips in a kiss after that, relishing the feel of our bare chests pressed against one another as I kept lazily fucking her with my fingers.

We didn't stop there, and I lost count of how many times she brought me to orgasm in the hours that followed. For each one she gave me, I ensured Blue Feather had one to match it, a ritual we kept up until we were both completely spent. Only then did we succumb to our exhaustion, and the last thing I remembered doing before darkness claimed me was tracing that soft feather between my fingers while Blue Feather hummed a melancholy melody.

The cold woke me long before my body was ready. Even as my mind emerged from the dream I could no longer remember, my body fought against it, curling in on itself as I fought in vain to get warm. A violent shiver finally pushed me over the edge, and I shot upright, clutching my aching arm and blinking in the... *blue* morning light?

No. Not morning, at least not quite, judging from the frost that had settled over the surrounding foliage. It had melted in some places, which told me dawn was close. Just not close enough to overshadow the glow of those luminescent flowers, which shone almost brighter now that they were coated in a thin layer of ice. Blue Feather had said they were sacred—was this why? And what had she said they were called, again?

Blue Feather.

I inhaled sharply, whirling around at the same time, and there she was. She slept curled on her side, but unlike me, she appeared completely at peace. Her long black hair swept out behind her while that swallow's feather, now draped over her cheek and nose, swayed back and forth in time with her deep, even breaths. She was covered, but not dressed, and had utilized her clothing as a blanket, bloodied and ruined as it was. One arm was stretched in my direction—her right—and only then did I vaguely recall a weight draped over me in my slumber. Had she... held me? Had I let her?

There wasn't time to examine how I felt about that before Blue Feather began to stir. A noise somewhere between a groan and a yawn escaped her as she arched her back and stretched, which caused the clothing to fall away from her breasts... *Fuck. Don't look.* Averting my gaze did little to stop my imagination from running wild, especially given what we'd done mere hours ago, but I refused to turn back until she'd stopped squirming around.

Her lips parted upon glimpsing me, and then of all things, she giggled. Heat crept to my cheeks, and when I snapped, it was harsher than I intended. "What the fuck is funny?"

She had to purse her lips to keep from bursting into another fit of laughter. "Aren't you cold?"

"Of course I am. Aren't *you* cold?"

"Not as cold as you, because my clothes are here. Not all the way over there." Blue Feather pointed, and my heart sank; not only was she right, I was topless. Muttering a string of curses under my breath, I scrambled over to my shirt before yanking it back on, wincing a little when it grazed my wounded arm. Something else tumbled from the fabric, something heavy enough to land with a dull *thud*: my dagger.

I stared at it for a while but ultimately decided against picking it up, especially after I noticed Blue Feather's reaction. She sat up and frowned, pulling her own shirt closer to her still-naked chest as she eyed me warily. "Why are you still looking at me like you want to kill me?"

I snorted. "Don't tell me the feeling isn't mutual."

"I'm not sure I know what that means."

The genuine confusion etched onto her face was all that kept me from snapping at her again. "It means," I started, pausing to choose my words carefully, "that yes, I still want to kill you, just… slightly less now, I suppose. And I assume the same is true for you. That's what 'mutual' means."

She narrowed her gaze but nodded without saying anything.

"Where did you learn English, anyway?" There hadn't been time to wonder in the whirlwind that these past several days had been, but now, my curiosity bubbled to the surface. "Did you pick it up just from watching us? The pirates?"

It was her turn to shoot me a harsh glare, which she kept up even as she began to put her own top back on. "Why do you keep doing that?"

"Doing what?"

"Ask questions that make me think you care, either before or after you've just told me you want to kill me. *Again.*"

I opened my mouth, then snapped it shut. I'd been about to blurt out that I *did* care, but was that the truth? And why did she care whether I did or didn't?

Before I could conjure up a response, Blue Feather had leaped to her feet, donned her pants in a huff, and went searching for her bow and dagger. Once she had both in hand, she gestured to where my weapon still lay in the dirt. "Keep that, but"—she made a face—"clean it before you use it for anything else."

She began to stalk away, and a sudden panic seized my chest. "Wait," I called after her, scrambling upright. Blue Feather halted but didn't turn around.

"I'm… sorry." It took effort to utter those simple words; not because I didn't mean them, but because I truly did. "I know I've been harsh to and with you, and not all of it was justified. You've been kind, despite having every reason not to be. And you can go. We both should. But before you do… why?"

She glanced over her shoulder, and her voice was barely louder than a whisper. "Why what, Elvira?"

"Why did you spare me?"

A long, heavy silence, but eventually, Blue Feather turned around. "You wanted to die. I wanted to show you how to live."

I'm not sure what I'd been expecting, but it certainly wasn't that. Tears pricked at the corner of my eyes, but not because of what Blue Feather had said—because of the reality I was now forced to acknowledge. For days, I'd been running from Cedric and his inevitable death, but now… I sucked in a deep breath.

Now, I had to face it.

Bowing my head, I mumbled a quick goodbye before darting away. Before I'd gotten two steps, however, Blue Feather was suddenly in front of me, and she threw out her arm to keep me from slamming into her.

"Not only was that a shitty farewell," she said, annoyance flashing in her gaze, "but… I think I can help you one last time."

I stifled an incredulous scoff and moved to sidestep her. "Thanks, but no thanks. 'Help me' any more, and I'll be owing you all sorts of—"

"It's about Cedric," she said, and I stilled.

"You… can help Cedric?"

"I can if he's alive."

I nodded, mostly because I couldn't bear imagining that he wasn't.

"Then we have to move quickly, and we have to leave now."

Several hours later, I was once again out of breath. It was all I could do to keep up as Blue Feather led the way through the dense forest, and she still hadn't told me where we were going. I may not know this part of Neverland well, but if we were headed back into pirate territory, surely we'd have arrived by now.

"How much farther?" I dared to ask when I could take the maddening silence no longer. After yesterday's Nightstalker attack, it felt like suicide to go traipsing through the forest as loudly as we were, but Blue Feather seemed to know exactly what she was doing and where we were going.

"Not much," she replied, still not bothering to slow her pace. "We're almost there."

It was at least twenty minutes more before we stopped, but right as I was about to complain again, we came across a large marked tree. In addition to a handful of symbols carved into its bark, that familiar luminescent paint coated several of its lower branches, emitting a dim light.

Blue Feather stepped up beside it, resting a hand on its trunk before turning to face me. "This," she said, nodding toward the tree, "is your way out of Neverland."

My mouth fell open, and I blinked in disbelief. "What? I thought we were saving Ced—"

"We are," Blue Feather pressed. "Well, you are. He's very sick, yes? What he needs can't be found in Neverland. You'll have to go to Afterport for the proper medicine, but this tree will lead you there. Follow the nizhano paint."

I glanced at the tree, then Blue Feather, and back again, and several things clicked at once, but it took a moment for me to find the words. "This is how you know English. You can... *leave*."

She nodded slowly. "I learned the language long before the curse struck, but yes. My people can come and go as we please. But we cannot stay long in Afterport, or any other place beyond this forest. Anyone born in Neverland must remain in Neverland, else they'll age and die."

I'd read as much in Jamie's letters, but it was another thing entirely hearing it from Blue Feather's lips. It must be true, then: time stopped in Neverland, meaning its inhabitants were more or less immortal so long as they kept up with the curse's demands. And that meant…

"Blue Feather," I asked quietly, my voice barely louder than a whisper. "How old are you?"

She wasn't listening or even looking at me, and she drew and nocked her bow so fast I hardly saw her move. "Get behind me," she hissed, and when I didn't immediately obey, she darted in front of me herself.

"Fuck," I spat, drawing my dagger the moment my mind caught up. "More Nightstalkers?"

"I don't know, but shut up."

We waited in tense silence, not daring to move a muscle even as the rustling of leaves and snapping of twigs grew louder. I held my breath, heart pounding in my chest, until a figure emerged from between two trees at the edge of our clearing.

Scarlett stepped into the light, her dark hair wild and her eyes wide with fear. She looked at me, then Blue Feather, then back again, but before either of us could say anything, Blue Feather had already drawn back her bowstring and aimed it directly at Scarlett's chest. I reacted instinctively, yanking at Blue Feather's arm and forcing her to fire at the ground.

She snapped something at me in her native language, but I had already leaped in front of her, blocking her access to Scarlett. "Don't shoot," I warned Blue Feather. "She's—"

"I know who she is," Blue Feather said, curling her lip. "Why is she *here*?"

I turned then, my own blood roaring in my ears as I forced the question burning in my chest. "Cedric. Is… Is he…?"

"He's alive," Scarlett murmured, still fixated on Blue Feather. "For now, at least."

Relief flooded through me, and I exhaled deeply, closing my eyes. There was still time, still a chance to save my brother, all thanks to Blue Feather. Gods, I owed her far more than a favor at this point, and so did—

"Why are you here?" Blue Feather demanded again, yanking me from my thoughts and prompting me to turn around. "How long have you been following us?"

Scarlett gripped my arm, speaking for my ears alone. "And your friend is…?"

"Blue Feather. Answer her before she shoots you."

Scarlett raised an arm in surrender, choosing her words carefully. "I only followed the noise. I didn't realize it was you until just now, Elvira. To be honest, after you didn't come back… I thought the forest had claimed you.

"Which was why I was out here, searching for a way out, just like I told you I would, and I overheard your plan."

My breath hitched as I realized where this was going, and I bit back a curse.

"If you're leaving Neverland," Scarlett said firmly, meeting my gaze, "then I'm coming with you."

It felt as if we'd gone back in time to several days ago, when we'd argued about this very thing over Cedric's unconscious body, and the last thing I wanted to do was waste precious time and energy doing it again. I shook my head slowly, a warning in my tone as I fought to keep my temper in check. "As I said before: *no*. One of us needs to stay here—"

"And why is that?" Scarlett's voice had risen to a shout. "We're both here now, so why can't we both go?"

"You'd leave Cedric to die alone?"

"You left him to die, period!"

"I won't help you run. I won't," I snapped, holding up a hand as Blue Feather took a step toward Scarlett and me. "If you want to flee this place, to flee him, fine, but find some other way."

Scarlett looked as though I'd slapped her, and for the first time, I noticed the tears streaming down her face. She sank to her knees, quietly sobbing, and a twinge of guilt gnawed at my chest. Scarlett *never* cried.

"Stop that," I hissed, but when she didn't, I knelt beside her. "You're making a scene."

"You don't understand," she whispered, and for some reason, her words sent chills down my spine. That's when she looked at me, her eyes red and swollen, and confessed the truth at last.

"I'm pregnant."

THE END... BUT JUST FOR NOW!

If you followed my suggested reading guide (found at the start of this novella), Elvira and Blue Feather's story continues in *A Forest of Blackened Trees*.

Available now at all major retailers!

https://books2read.com/afobt

For another free short story, exclusive bonus excerpts, news, and discounts, make sure to sign up for R. L. Davennor's newsletter at:

https://rldavennor.com/newsletter

ABOUT THE AUTHOR

Raelynn Davennor (she/they) writes fantasy romance and fairytale retellings—usually of the darker variety—and is the author of the Curses of Never and The Phantom of Notre Dame series, both of which became viral BookTok hits.

She is known for her diverse and morally complex characters, as well as her ability to craft heart-wrenching plots that explore heavy themes. While she is a firm believer that light cannot be fully appreciated without first traveling through heaps of darkness, Raelynn always ensures that her characters find their well-deserved happily ever afters—especially the LGBTQ+ ones.

When not obsessing over her latest idea, she enjoys pampering her menagerie of pets and pretending she isn't an adult.

Her home base is https://rldavennor.com where you'll find more information, her newsletter, and links to social media.